SPLASH!

Anna landed flat on her stomach in the water.

Walter wiped away the water that had splashed into his face. "What a belly flop!"

"*That's* a dive?" said Otis.

Anna came up smiling. "How'd I do?"

"Great!" said Grandpa Walt. He gave her a thumbs-up sign. "Try again. Remember, squeeze your arms tight against your ears."

Walter stared at Grandpa Walt. "She'll never win," he said.

Grandpa Walt took Walter and Otis aside. "Not everyone can win, boys. The goal for athletes like Anna is to do their best, not just to win."

Walter watched Anna try another dive. She belly flopped again. "Doesn't she get tired?" he asked. "Why doesn't she just quit?"

Grandpa Walt wiped his face with a towel. "Anna is a true athlete. She doesn't give up. She's a *real* winner."

Other Bantam Skylark Books you will enjoy
Ask your bookseller for the books you have
    missed

THE NEVER SINK NINE

Olympic Otis

BY GIBBS DAVIS

Illustrated by
George Ulrich

A BANTAM SKYLARK BOOK®
NEW YORK • TORONTO • LONDON • SYDNEY • AUCKLAND

RL 2, 005–008

OLYMPIC OTIS
A Bantam Skylark Book / May 1993

ISBN 0-553-48078-2

Published simultaneously in the United States and Canada

Bantam Books are published by Bantam Books, a division of Bantam
Doubleday Dell Publishing Group, Inc. Its trademark, consisting of the
words "Bantam Books" and the portrayal of a rooster, is Registered in
U.S. Patent and Trademark Office and in other countries. Marca
Registrada. Bantam Books, 1540 Broadway, New York, New York
10036.

PRINTED IN THE UNITED STATES OF AMERICA

OPM 0 9 8 7 6 5 4 3 2 1

To all the Special Olympics athletes and their families, and to all the volunteers who help keep the program going.

"Special Olympics is sport in its truest sense. The goal is not to win, but to try. To experience, not to conquer. No time is too slow, no distance too small to earn a ribbon, a hug, a cheer, or a sincere 'well done.' No records are broken in Special Olympics except those for courage, determination, and sportsmanship."
Eunice Kennedy Shriver
From a speech to Special Olympics
athletes, 1985

Special thanks to: Ms. Janet Riley, Director of Special Olympics, New York Chapter, and Ms. Karin Hawley, Area Director, Special Olympics, Milwaukee, Wisconsin.

Contents

CHAPTER ONE

Project Partners

Walter was thinking about baseball. He opened his desk. His Never Sink Nine baseball cap was still there. It was right on top of his book for reading class, *Stories from Around the World.*

He pulled out the skinny easy reader and covered it with a fat library book. He looked around to make sure none of the other third graders had seen. Walter hated Reading Hour. It made him feel dumb.

"Dumb, dumb, dumb, dumb, dumb," he said five times for luck.

Walter pulled out his baseball cap and put it on backward, the way he always did. He felt smarter right away.

"No hats in class, Walter," said Mrs. Howard. Walter's teacher walked back to his desk. "Where's your book of folktales?"

Walter shrugged. "I forgot it." Walter's ears burned. He didn't like lying to Mrs. Howard. But he couldn't let anyone see him with a baby book.

"This book looks hard for you," said Mrs. Howard. "Need some help?"

Walter shook his head. "I need my hat. It helps me read better."

"Okay," said Mrs. Howard with a smile. "But after Reading Hour it comes off."

Walter's best friend, Mike Lasky, looked at Walter's cap.

"Lucky," Mike whispered from across the aisle. He blew a big bubble of pink gum. Mike only chewed the kind that came with baseball cards.

Walter grinned back at his friend. He

inched closer to the desk in front of him. A bag of toy horses hung from the back of Melissa Nichols's chair. Walter gave it a little kick.

Melissa spun around. "Hey, watch it!" When she saw Walter's Never Sink Nine team cap she smiled. Melissa and Mike were members of the Never Sink Nine baseball team too.

"Psst!" Mike signaled to Walter. He was writing something on a piece of paper. He crumpled it into a ball and tossed it over to Walter.

Walter flattened it on his desk. The words were nice and short and easy to read. He turned the note so Melissa could read it too.

Every day their Never Sink Nine friend and classmate Pete Santos wrote a joke on the blackboard. And every day he hid the answer in a different place. Walter looked at today's joke.

MONDAY Pete's Joke
of the day
What time is it when Otis
sits in a chair?

Walter watched Otis Hooper sneak bites from a candy bar. A Never Sink Nine T-shirt stretched over his round stomach. Otis was the Never Sink Nine's catcher. He was almost ten years old. He was the biggest kid in the third grade, and the only one who had been left back.

"Look at me," Mike whispered to Walter. "I'm Otis." He puffed out his cheeks and stuck out his stomach.

Walter covered his mouth to keep from laughing out loud. He knew it was a mean

4

thing for Mike to say, but he thought it was funny anyway.

Mrs. Howard clapped her hands. "Reading Hour is over. Everyone line up. It's time to go to the nurse's office."

"How come?" asked Mike. His face turned pale under his freckles. "No one's sick."

"It's time for our class checkup," said Mrs. Howard. "The school nurse will weigh and measure everyone. Then you can go to lunch."

"No shots?" asked Melissa. She held a toy horse tight in one hand.

"No shots," said Mrs. Howard. "I promise."

Melissa pranced the toy horse across her desk top and raced to be first in line. Walter and Mike ran up to be second and third. Everyone else followed.

Mrs. Howard's class walked in a straight line to Mr. Mooney's office. Mr. Mooney was the school nurse.

"I'm first," said Melissa, kicking off her shoes. She stepped onto the scale to be weighed.

After Melissa was finished, Mr. Mooney let Melissa weigh her favorite toy horse, Misty. "Six ounces," said Mr. Mooney, making a note. "Same as last year."

Melissa passed Walter and Mike on her way out. "See you at lunch," she said, and cantered down the hall to the cafeteria.

"You're next," Mr. Mooney said to Walter. Walter was ready. He stepped onto the scale. "You've gained five pounds," said Mr. Mooney. "Good work."

Walter knew measuring his height came next. He took a deep breath and stood as tall as he could. He felt the measuring stick lightly touch the top of his head.

"Two-and-one-half inches taller," said Mr. Mooney. "You're shooting up like a weed, Walter."

Walter smiled so hard that his cheeks hurt. Not everyone could grow like a weed.

6

Walter waited for Mike to finish. Mike met him in the hall.

"I only grew half an inch," said Mike softly. He tugged at his patchy hair and sighed. "And I gained one lousy pound."

Walter punched his friend lightly on the arm. "You'll make up for it next year. Just eat more."

Mike's face lit up. He jogged toward the cafeteria. "Come on! I've got a lot of eating to do." Walter ran after him.

They found Melissa's table filling up with members of the Never Sink Nine. Pretty soon the whole Never Sink Nine team was sitting together at the same table.

"Nurse Mooney said I was the tallest in the whole class," said Pete proudly. He sat up straight.

"So what," grumbled Mike. "Who wants to be class beanpole?"

Walter knew Mike wished he were taller.

"We know who's the *biggest* in the class,"

Christy Chung whispered loudly. Otis sat at the end of the table. He stared down at his tray of food.

"He's the biggest because he was left back," Walter said.

"You should talk," said Melissa. "You're in the slow reading group."

"Everybody's being so mean today," Katie Kessler said.

Walter, Melissa, and Christy looked down at their trays. Christy's cheeks turned bright pink. "I'm sorry, Otis. I didn't mean to hurt your feelings."

Otis shrugged. "That's okay. I *am* the biggest kid in class."

Pete gave Otis a nudge. "How come you're not eating?"

Otis sighed. "Mr. Mooney says I have to go on a diet. He's calling my parents."

Everyone at the table moaned. None of them liked to have their parents called.

"My mom says it's just baby fat," said Otis. "All the Hoopers have big bones."

They all finished their lunches in silence. Walter looked at Otis staring sadly at his food and wondered how it felt to be fat.

After recess everyone went back to the classroom. Mrs. Howard had written ROCKVILLE COMMUNITY PROJECTS on the board in big letters. She put down her chalk and faced the class.

"This afternoon we're going to break up into pairs," said Mrs. Howard. "Then you and your partner will choose a community project to work on for the next two weeks."

Everyone started picking project partners.

Walter looked at Mike's empty desk. He was in the bathroom peeling bubble gum off his face. Suddenly Walter spotted Mrs. Howard walking down the aisle toward him with Otis. Walter pretended to lean over and tie his shoe. He looked down at Mrs. Howard's orange shoes with daisies on the toes and Otis's large sneakers.

"Walter," said Mrs. Howard, "I'd like you and Otis to work together."

Walter sat up. "But Mike and me are always partners!"

"Mike and *I* are always partners," corrected Mrs. Howard. "Mike can be someone else's partner this time," she said in a firm voice. "Now you and Otis work on finding a project that interests both of you."

Otis squeezed into Mike's desk and smiled at Walter. He pulled out paper and a pencil. "This is gonna be fun."

Walter glared at Otis. "Yeah, a barrel of monkeys."

When Mike returned to class he was paired with Melissa. Everyone had a project partner now. Mike and Melissa decided to start a paper recycling program for their neighborhood. Walter and Otis, though, couldn't agree on anything.

11

"How about collecting soda cans?" said Otis. "We could turn them in and donate the money."

"Forget it," said Walter. "I'm not dragging around a bag of cans."

The school bell rang. Walter looked at his Babe Ruth wristwatch. It was exactly three o'clock. School was over.

"I'm out of here," said Walter, putting on his Never Sink Nine cap. He grabbed his backpack and hurried outside.

Otis ran after him. "Mrs. Howard says we have to decide on our project by tomorrow!"

Walter stopped in front of the bike rack. A small crowd of kids was looking down at the ground and laughing. Walter pushed his way into the crowd. Some words were written in chalk on the asphalt.

"It's the answer to Pete's joke," someone said.

Pete's joke went through Walter's mind: *What time is it when Otis Hooper sits in a chair?* He looked at the answer.

Walter chuckled. "That's a good one." He jumped on his bike and pushed off. He caught up with Otis walking home. Walter slowed down beside him. "Did you see Pete's joke?"

Otis kicked a stone. "No," he mumbled. "It's just another fat joke."

Walter didn't know what to say. He had never thought about a joke hurting someone.

Otis looked at Walter. "I was in Mr. Chase's slow reading class for two years. It's not so bad. I could teach you some tricks."

"Thanks." Walter forced a smile. It was nice knowing another slow reader. "My mom went on a diet last year and lost a ton. I could ask her for some dieting tips."

"Okay," said Otis. He looked hopeful.

"Being skinny isn't so great anyway," said Walter. "Wait'll you can play football. No one makes jokes about big guys then."

Otis's face lit up. "Think so?"

"Sure," said Walter. Suddenly he had an idea. "I bet my Grandpa Walt'll come up with something for our community project. He coaches special kids at the YMCA every Monday."

"What makes 'em so special?" asked Otis.

Walter shrugged. "I'm meeting him at the Y. Wanna come?"

Otis nodded.

"Hop on," said Walter. He stood up on the bike pedals while Otis took the seat. *I wouldn't do this for anyone but another slow reader,* thought Walter.

Walter pushed off and started pedaling hard. It was tough going. Otis was heavier than he thought. He wondered how he'd ever make it through two whole weeks with his new project partner.

14

CHAPTER TWO

Assistant Coaches

Walter parked his bike in front of the YMCA. He collapsed on the grass and tried to catch his breath. "Otis, you're killing me."

"Sorry." Otis lifted himself off Walter's bike seat. "Guess I gained a few pounds."

"Try a *ton,*" Walter said. "Just teasing," he added quickly.

"Ha, ha," said Otis. He grabbed Walter's hand and pulled him up. "How come you think your grandpa knows a good project for us?"

"Grandpa Walt knows everything," said

Walter. "He's the only guy in Rockville who played in the minors *and* he's my grandfather."

"Wow," said Otis, following Walter inside.

Walter stopped in front of a desk piled high with towels. A man sat behind the desk reading magazines.

"Hi, Mr. Ackerman," said Walter.

Mr. Ackerman looked over his glasses at Walter and then at Otis. "Looks like you've brought a teammate."

Otis tugged at his Never Sink Nine cap. "We're project partners."

"What's your project?" asked Mr. Ackerman.

"We don't know yet," said Walter. "That's why we've got to see Grandpa Walt."

"Can't do it until four o'clock," said Mr. Ackerman. "Right now your grandpa's coaching the Special Olympics team."

"But it's important," said Walter. "Can't you let us in?"

"Ple-e-e-ease," said Otis.

Mr. Ackerman reached over and stamped the two boys' hands with a little purple fish. "Go on," he said, "before I change my mind." Usually Walter paid fifty cents and Mr. Ackerman gave him a towel. But today he wasn't swimming.

Walter opened the heavy door marked POOL.

Inside, the huge pool was filled with athletes swimming laps. A few older men and women were helping them.

"Boy, it smells in here," said Otis.

"Chlorine," said Walter. "You get used to it."

A large man with glasses waved at Walter. "Over here!" He was helping a girl in the shallow end of the pool.

Walter and Otis walked over to him.

"Hi, Coach," said Otis. Grandpa Walt was the Never Sink Nine's baseball coach. A dark-haired girl stood in the water next to Grandpa Walt.

"Boys, meet Anna Brink," said Grandpa Walt. "She's my star swimmer for the ten- to twelve-year-olds freestyle event."

The girl smiled up at Grandpa Walt. "I'm ten-and-a-half," she said proudly.

Walter didn't want to meet Anna. He had a project to find. "You've got to help us," said Walter. "Mrs. Howard says we have to find a community project by tomorrow."

"Yeah," said Otis. "By tomorrow."

"This takes some thought," said Grandpa. He floated in the water on his back. Suddenly he spurted a long stream of water in the air.

Anna giggled and slapped the water with her hands. "A whale! Coach is a whale!"

Grandpa Walt stood up. "I've got it. You and Otis can be my assistant coaches for the Rockville Special Olympics Meet. They'll be coming up a week from Saturday."

Walter and Otis looked at each other. "Assistant coaches!" they said together.

18

"Do I get a whistle?" asked Otis.

"What about a 'Coach' T-shirt?" said Walter.

Grandpa Walt pulled himself out of the water and stood beside them. "Yes, but your job is to encourage the special athletes in training," he said firmly.

"What's so special about them?" asked Otis.

"They're slow," Walter whispered to Otis.

Grandpa Walt frowned. "Special means they're people with mental retardation. Anna was born with Down's syndrome. She has a harder time learning things than you boys do."

Anna got out of the pool. She tugged on Grandpa Walt's arm. "Watch me dive."

Anna put her hands together over her head and leaned over the deep end of the pool.

SPLASH!

20

She landed flat on her stomach in the water.

Walter wiped the water that had splashed onto his face. His shirt was soaked. "What a belly flop!"

"*That's* a dive?" said Otis.

Anna came up smiling. She pushed her wet bangs out of her eyes. "How'd I do?"

"Great!" said Grandpa Walt. He gave her a thumbs-up sign. "Try again. Remember, squeeze your arms tight against your ears and point down toward the bottom of the pool."

Walter stared at Grandpa Walt. "She'll never win a race," he said.

Grandpa Walt took Walter and Otis aside. "Not everyone can win, boys. The goal for athletes like Anna is to do their best, not just to win."

Walter watched Anna try another dive. She belly flopped again. "Doesn't she get tired?" he asked. "Why doesn't she just quit?"

21

Grandpa Walt wiped his face with a towel and watched Anna try again. "Anna is a true athlete. She doesn't give up. She's a *real* winner."

Walter nodded, but he didn't understand.

"She's fat, like me," said Otis softly.

"A lot of famous athletes are big," said Grandpa Walt. "Think of Babe Ruth."

Walter looked at his Babe Ruth wristwatch. He had never thought of the Babe as heavy, but he was.

"Can I be a special athlete too?" asked Otis.

"Afraid not," said Grandpa Walt. "Only athletes with mental retardation can be in the Special Olympics. But you can train with me. I swim fifty laps every morning. I'll pick you up before school. Deal?"

Otis's face lit up. "Deal."

Walter was beginning to feel left out. "Can I train too?"

"Sure, Slugger." Grandpa Walt put one arm around Walter and the other around Otis. "The three of us will go into training."

Anna came running toward Grandpa Walt. She gave him a big, wet hug. "Me too!" she said.

"All this hugging reminds me that there's another job you can do," Grandpa Walt said to the boys. "You can also be official huggers."

"Huggers?" Walter made a face.

"Huggers congratulate each athlete at the end of a race," said Grandpa Walt. "You can do it with a hug, a handshake, or a high five."

"Hug!" said Otis.

"Handshake," said Walter. He wasn't sure he wanted to hug someone in public he wasn't related to.

No one had to ask Anna which she liked best. She was hugging Grandpa Walt as tight as she could.

"Wait'll we tell everyone about our community project," said Otis.

"Being an assistant coach sure beats collecting soda cans," said Walter. He held up one hand for a high five with his new project partner.

CHAPTER THREE

Camping Out

Friday afternoon a tall man named Mr. Chase poked his head inside Mrs. Howard's classroom. He waved to get Walter's attention. Mr. Chase was the school reading teacher. Twice a week Walter joined six other students in the resource room for reading class.

Walter hid his skinny book under one arm and hurried down the hall. Reading was hard work, but Mr. Chase always made it fun.

Today Mr. Chase greeted everyone at the door. *"Konnichiwa,"* he said and bowed deeply at the waist. "That means hello in Japanese." He was wearing a long red-silk coat over his clothes. He called it a *kimono*.

Mr. Chase pulled down the world map and pointed to a group of islands. "Japan," he said. "This is where we're traveling today. Did you all remember to bring your passports?"

Walter held up the passport he had made in Mr. Chase's class. It had a small snapshot of himself. It was already stamped *Africa* and *Greece*. Walter felt like a real world traveler.

Mr. Chase stamped all the passports with *Japan* and the date. Then they all opened their copies of *Stories from Around the World* and read the Japanese story together. Then Mr. Chase asked them questions about what they had read. When they were finished Mr. Chase stamped everyone's passport again. Walter knew that meant they were leaving Japan.

"Did any of you finish reading a book on your own this week?" asked Mr. Chase.

All the students raised their hands except Walter and another boy. Walter wanted to explain that he didn't have time to read this week. He was too busy helping train Special Olympics athletes.

"Good work," said Mr. Chase. He passed out gold stars to everyone who had raised a hand.

Walter watched a girl named Nicole take her new star. She pressed it onto a worksheet filled with shiny gold stars.

"I have ten stars," said Nicole. "How many do you have?"

Walter covered his worksheet. "None of your beeswax."

"It doesn't matter how many stars you have," said Mr. Chase, "as long as you keep trying."

Walter peeked at his two measly stars. *Mr. Chase is wrong,* he thought. *Stars do matter.* Walter wanted a whole page of them. Then he would feel smart.

After school Walter stuffed *Stories from Around the World* in the bottom of his backpack and pulled on his Never Sink Nine cap. He hurried outside to the bike rack. To-night was special. He and his older brother, Danny, were going to camp out in the back-yard.

Walter pedaled double-time all the way home. He pulled into the driveway next to Grandpa Walt's station wagon. Every Friday night Grandpa Walt came to dinner.

"I'm ho-o-o-ome!" Walter shouted, fling-ing open the front door. He ran right into someone.

"Oof!"

Walter looked straight into Otis's round face. "What're *you* doing here?"

"While you were at reading class, me and Anna were training at the Y," said Otis. "Coach invited us to dinner."

Walter sniffed the air. Otis smelled like chlorine and his hair was still wet.

Anna came out of the kitchen with Grandpa Walt.

"Hi, Slugger," said Grandpa Walt. He was wearing a Special Olympics T-shirt.

28

Anna ran up and gave Walter a bear hug. Her dark hair tickled his face. "Hi," she said.

"Where's Danny?" asked Walter, letting Anna hug him. He didn't have time to talk. He was going camping.

"In there." Otis pointed toward the den.

Danny was sitting in front of the TV.

"Come on," Walter said to Danny. "We have to put up the tent before it gets dark."

"Forget it," said Danny. "There's a good movie on TV tonight."

"You promised!" said Walter.

"I changed my mind," said Danny. "Camping in the backyard is for babies."

"You did it last year," said Walter.

Danny looked at Walter. "I'm ten now. Get lost, turkey brain."

Walter stared at his brother. He felt like crying. He picked up a pillow from the couch and threw it at him. Danny dodged it and kept on watching TV.

Walter walked into the kitchen and collapsed on a chair. Grandpa Walt, Otis, and Anna were helping Mrs. Dodd make dinner.

"What's the matter, Walter?" asked Mrs. Dodd.

"Danny won't camp out with me," said Walter.

"That's too bad, honey," said Mrs. Dodd.

Grandpa Walt sat down next to Walter. "You know, Danny isn't the only camper around."

Walter sat up. "You mean *you'll* camp out with me?"

Grandpa Walt smiled and shook his head. "My bowling league meets tonight. But I bet Otis would like camping."

Walter looked over at Otis mashing potatoes in a big bowl. He dipped a finger in the potatoes and stuck it in his mouth. "He'll hog all the room in the tent," whispered Walter.

Grandpa Walt nudged him. "Why don't you give Otis a chance? It's no fun camping alone."

30

"I guess it's too late to call Mike," said Walter. He thought about sleeping in the backyard all alone in the dark. "Hey Otis, wanna camp out with me tonight?" Walter shouted across the kitchen.

"Sure!" Otis smiled. "I'll ask my mom." Otis called his mother on the phone and got her permission to sleep over. "No problem," he said, hanging up the phone.

Grandpa Walt helped Walter and Otis set up camp in the backyard until Mrs. Dodd called them in to dinner.

Everyone sat down to a dinner of roast chicken, mashed potatoes, stuffing, brussels sprouts, and buttered rolls.

Danny looked across the table at Otis with disgust. "Walter's friend is *drooling*."

Mrs. Dodd frowned at Danny. "Danny, that's not nice. He's not really drooling. He's just a little bit hungry."

"I'm in training," said Otis sadly. He was staring at the bowl of mashed potatoes.

31

"Me too," said Anna.

"Athletes have to make sacrifices," said Mr. Dodd.

Grandpa Walt nodded in agreement. "The Rockville Area Special Olympics Meet is coming up next week. We have to get in shape."

After they had finished eating, Mrs. Dodd stood up. "I was going to make a chocolate cake for dessert tonight," she said, going into the kitchen.

Otis and Anna let out a big groan.

Mrs. Dodd came out of the kitchen carrying a big bowl of fruit salad. "But in honor of our athletes-in-training I made a lovely fruit salad instead."

This time Danny and Walter groaned.

After dinner Grandpa Walt said good night and got ready to take Anna home. Walter and Otis waved good-bye from the driveway.

Grandpa Walt poked his head out the car window. "Don't forget to invite your friends to the meet next Saturday. And tell everyone from the Never Sink Nine that I want to take them to Pizza Palace for dinner afterward!''

''See you at the pool tomorrow, Anna!'' shouted Otis.

''Let's get in the tent,'' said Walter, heading for the backyard. He couldn't wait one second longer. ''We're sleeping in our clothes,'' he said.

''Wow,'' said Otis, following behind. ''This is great.''

They opened the pup tent flap and got into their sleeping bags. They wiggled partway outside the tent so they could look up at the sky.

''There's the Big Dipper,'' said Otis, pointing up. ''It's part of my favorite constellation. If you squint, the stars around the Big Dipper look like a bear.'' He showed Walter how to draw an imaginary line between the stars to make a picture.

Then Otis pointed to the brightest spot in the sky, near the horizon. "That's the planet Venus. It's always easy to find."

Walter thought about how Otis knew the names of stars and planets. "You're not so dumb," he said.

"Thanks," said Otis.

"Let's wish on a star," said Walter. "But don't say it out loud or it won't come true." Walter picked a little twinkling star right above his house. "I wish all the stars in the sky were gold stars on my reading worksheet," he whispered to himself. He knew Otis wished he were thin.

"I've got a joke," said Otis. "What kind of tent barks like a dog?" He looked at Walter. "Give up?"

Walter nodded. He loved jokes.

"A *pup* tent!" said Otis.

Walter laughed. "Good one."

Otis started to bark like a puppy and Walter joined in. They barked and laughed until they were worn out. No one told them to be quiet. *It's fun camping out with Otis,* thought Walter.

"Let's make hand shadows with our flashlights," said Otis. They sat inside the tent and made animal shadows on the tent walls.

After a while, Otis yawned and crawled back inside his sleeping bag. "Time to hit the sack," he said.

Walter pulled two dirty blue socks out of his pillow case. "My lucky socks," he said, putting them on. Grandpa Walt gave them to him, and Walter always wore them at baseball games and on special occasions.

"They sure *smell* lucky," said Otis.

"Thanks," said Walter. "I haven't washed them once all baseball season." Walter snuggled down into his sleeping bag. " 'Night," he said.

"What're you gonna dream about?" asked Otis.

"I dunno," said Walter. "Maybe hitting a home run. What are you gonna dream about?"

Otis sighed. "Eating two big pieces of chocolate cake." He closed his eyes and rolled over.

Walter looked out the tent flap and saw a light on inside the house. Camping out was a little scary, but the light made him feel safe. Walter closed his eyes. He listened to Otis's stomach rumble until he fell asleep.

CHAPTER FOUR

Stars and Candy Bars

The next week flew by for Walter and Otis. They spent every day after school at the Y helping Anna improve her diving skills. It was their job to make sure each athlete had swimming goggles and a clean towel. But most of all they helped make sure everyone had fun.

By Thursday Walter couldn't wait to tell everyone about his community project. The Rockville Special Olympics Meet was just two days away.

"Who wants to tell the class how their

community project is coming along?" asked Mrs. Howard.

A few hands shot up. Mrs. Howard nodded toward Walter's friend, Mike Lasky. "Mike, you go first."

Mike hid his gum and stood up. "You all know that Melissa and I started a paper drive. We asked everyone in our neighborhood to tie up their newspapers and drop them off at the Rockville recycling center. Some people can't, so our job is to pick them up in Melissa's little sister's wagon." He took a bow and sat down.

"Very good," said Mrs. Howard. "Tony, tell us how your newsletter is doing."

Tony Pappas stopped doodling on a piece of paper and stood up. He was always drawing. "Pete and I decided to call the newsletter the *Rockville Rookie Report*. Our first issue's going to cover our class community projects."

"Wonderful!" said Mrs. Howard. "I'll look forward to reading the first issue." She looked at the clock. "We have time for one more before recess."

Walter waved his hand in the air. Mrs. Howard nodded in his direction. Walter stood up and suddenly felt very nervous. "My project partner is Otis." His mind went blank. It was scary standing up in front of everyone.

Otis gave Walter a thumbs-up sign.

Walter took a deep breath. "We're assistant coaches for Special Olympics athletes. There's an area meet this Saturday and we're inviting everyone to come. It starts at ten o'clock at the YMCA."

"Tell us a little about Special Olympics, Otis," said Mrs. Howard.

Otis stood up. "Special Olympics gives people with mental retardation a chance to compete in sports and feel good about themselves. They play all kinds of sports like we do: swimming, track, basketball, and soccer. There are Special Olympics games all over the world, just like the other Olympics."

"Yeah," said Walter, smiling at Otis. He knew Otis had been reading up on Special Olympics at the library. It wasn't so bad having Otis as a project partner after all. Walter and Otis sat down together.

"Aren't mentally retarded people just dumb?" asked Mike.

"No," said Mrs. Howard. "They learn in a different way. But they are people who have feelings just like you and me."

The school bell rang for recess.

"Come on," said Walter, leading the way outside. "I've got something important to tell everyone."

The Never Sink Nine met by the swings on the playground. Melissa started lining up her toy horses on the ground. Tony sat in a swing drawing a picture.

Walter waited until all of his baseball teammates were there. Some of them were wearing Never Sink Nine team caps.

"What's up?" asked Katie Kessler.

"Grandpa Walt wants everybody to come to the Special Olympics this Saturday," said Walter.

"Why?" asked Christy.

Walter shrugged. "It'll be fun. And Grandpa Walt is taking us out for pizza afterward. Can I count on everybody to show up?"

"Christy and I will be there," said Melissa. "And I'll tell Jenny." Jenny was Melissa's little sister.

"I'm in," said Mike. Then he blew a big bubble of gum. Everyone else nodded.

After the meeting Mike gave Walter a nudge. "Wanna go to Klugman's Pharmacy after school? They just got in some new water pistols."

"Sure," said Walter. He hadn't seen much of Mike since they had begun their community projects. He missed his friend.

After school Walter and Mike bicycled into downtown Rockville to Klugman's Pharmacy.

"The new pistols are in back," said Mike, leading the way.

Walter followed him slowly. He stopped to look at pencils with funny erasers, neon orange notepads, and sheets of stickers. There were stickers of animals, sports teams, and gold stars.

Gold stars!

Walter's heart beat fast. He reached out and touched the shiny gold stars. They were exactly like the ones on his reading worksheet. Only there were hundreds of them! Walter grabbed a sheet of stars off the rack.

I can't let anyone see me, thought Walter, hurrying toward the checkout counter. He thought of covering his whole reading worksheet with stars. More stars than Nicole, more than anyone.

"Oof!"

Walter bumped into someone and his stickers fell to the ground. He looked up into

Otis's surprised face. Otis was carrying two big fists full of candy bars.

"What're *you* doing here!" demanded Walter.

"It's a free country," said Otis loudly. He looked at the sheet of gold stars on the ground. "I tried that. It didn't work. It's not the same as when Mr. Chase gives you one."

Walter picked up the stickers. He knew Otis was right. All the gold stars in Klugman's wouldn't be worth one of Mr. Chase's.

Walter looked at Otis's waist. Something was different. "You look thinner," said Walter.

"I pulled my belt in another notch today," said Otis with a sigh. Slowly he put each candy bar back in its box. "Coach was right. It's tough being an athlete. I miss my candy bars."

Walter nodded.

"See you at the Y," said Otis, and he waved good-bye.

44

Walter walked back to the stickers rack and returned the sheet of stars. *The only way I can put stars on my worksheet is to read,* he thought. It was as simple as that.

CHAPTER FIVE

Opening Ceremony

Saturday morning Walter was late. It took him an hour to find his lucky socks. He found them in the bottom of his sleeping bag.

Walter pedaled extra hard to the YMCA.

"Hurry, hurry, hurry, hurry, hurry," he said, five times for luck. He didn't want to miss the Opening Ceremony.

Hundreds of cars were parked in front of the Y. He had never seen it so packed. A huge blue-and-yellow banner stretched across the front of the building: WELCOME ROCKVILLE AREA SPECIAL OLYMPICS.

"Wow," said Walter. He followed the arrows pointing to the track field behind the building. A big crowd was already gathered for the Opening Ceremony.

"Over here, Walter!" Otis stood on the bleachers waving his Never Sink Nine cap.

Walter ran to join Otis and his teammates. They were all wearing their blue Never Sink Nine baseball caps. Even Homer the goat, their team mascot, was wearing one.

"Thanks for coming," Walter said. Homer butted him gently and licked his hand.

Mike looked at Walter's T-shirt. SPECIAL OLYMPICS, ROCKVILLE, ASSISTANT COACH was printed on the front. "You and Otis are sure lucky to be coaches."

"*Assistant* coaches," corrected Grandpa Walt, walking up behind them. "*I'm* the coach." He gave Mike a wink and smiled.

Walter turned around and gave Grandpa Walt a big hug. Otis gave him a hug too.

48

"I knew you and Otis would make good huggers," said Grandpa Walt.

"Huggers?" said Melissa, making a face.

Some of Walter's friends giggled.

Walter felt himself getting mad. "Huggers have an important job," he said loudly. "We get to congratulate the athletes at the end of their races."

"Yeah," said Otis, backing him up. "Or we can do it with a handshake or a high five."

"Walter!" Anna ran through the crowd. She tugged at Walter's jacket. "Did you bring them?"

Walter pulled his lucky socks out of his jacket pocket and handed them to Anna.

"P.U.!" said Melissa, pinching her nose. "You're not going to wear his stinky old socks, are you?"

"These are special *lucky* socks," said Anna. She sat down on the ground and took off her sneakers. She pulled on the dirty socks and smiled.

49

Walter crossed his arms and faced Melissa. "If you knew anything, you'd know the smellier they get, the luckier they get."

Melissa rolled her eyes.

Anna pulled her sneakers on over the dirty socks. "Thanks, Coach," she said to Walter.

Walter smiled. No one had ever called him Coach before.

Suddenly music started playing over the loudspeaker. Groups of Special Olympics athletes began marching around the track. They were all dressed alike and were waving big blue banners with the Special Olympics logo. Some of them read: SKILL, COURAGE, SHARING, JOY.

"The Parade of Athletes is starting!" said Grandpa Walt. "Hurry, Anna. You don't want to miss it."

Anna pulled up Walter's lucky socks. She grabbed a banner and joined the parade.

Walter watched Anna march by wearing his lucky socks. He felt proud.

"Mike, look. It's your dad." Walter pointed high into the bleachers. Officer Lasky was easy to spot in his blue police uniform.

Walter saw a lot of people he knew in the crowd. Mrs. Howard stood next to Mr. Chase with most of their third grade class. Mr. and Mrs. Klugman from Klugman's Pharmacy were there, and so was Mr. Swenson from the sporting goods store. Mrs. Miller, the traffic crossing guard, was there, still in her neon orange jacket.

"Boy, Special Olympics meets sure bring everybody together," said Otis.

Mike and Walter nodded.

Walter spotted his brother, Danny, with his friend Joey Cooke. Walter couldn't believe his eyes. He pushed through the crowd to Danny.

"Thanks for coming," Walter said to his brother.

Danny shrugged and kept watching the parade. "I didn't have anything better to do."

Walter knew it wasn't true. Danny was missing all his favorite Saturday-morning TV shows.

After the Parade of Athletes, the flag was raised and everyone sang "The Star-Spangled Banner." Then a runner carried the Special Olympics torch around the track and lit the Flame of Hope.

"Wow," said Mike. "This is cool."

"Told you," said Walter. He felt proud to be a part of the Special Olympics.

"The oath is next," said Otis.

Everyone recited the Special Olympics oath. Walter and Otis knew it by heart.

" 'Let me win, but if I cannot win, let me be brave in the attempt,' " said Walter and Otis together.

Hundreds of yellow and blue balloons rose into the air above the track field. Everyone looked up at the sky filled with balloons and "oohed" and "aahed."

Walter turned to Otis. "Looks like it's time for the games to begin, Coach." Walter held up a hand.

Otis slapped Walter's hand in a high five. "I'm with you, Coach."

Otis and Walter jogged inside together. They had important work to do.

CHAPTER SIX

Everyone's a Winner

The locker room was crowded. Special Olympics athletes and volunteers were changing into swim gear.

Walter stepped out of his jeans and admired his swim trunks. They had tiny baseball bats and gloves on them.

"Ready?" said Otis.

Walter looked at Otis's swim trunks. They were covered with pictures of ice-cream cones.

"I can't eat sweets," said Otis, "but I can wear them."

Walter nodded. "You've lost weight."

"Three pounds," said Otis. He smoothed his Assistant Coach T-shirt over his stomach.

The bleachers were full of people when Walter and Otis entered the pool room. The races were about to begin.

"Every coach needs a whistle," said Grandpa Walt. He hung a red plastic whistle around each boy's neck. "Don't use them until you're outside," he warned.

Walter touched the red whistle. He couldn't wait to try it.

"Okay, assistant coaches, do your jobs." Grandpa Walt put a hand on each boy's shoulder. "Our athletes need encouragement. Remember, the main thing is to try, and to do one's best. Now have fun!"

Walter and Otis went to work. They helped congratulate swimmers at the finish line and got them dry towels. Walter was so busy he almost missed Anna's event.

"Ten- to twelve-year-olds in the fifty-meter freestyle, take your places!'' boomed the loudspeaker.

Walter dropped an armful of towels. ''That's Anna's race!''

Walter found Anna sitting on the bleachers with Otis. He was giving her last-minute advice on diving.

''Bend at the waist and keep your arms together over your head,'' said Otis, with a serious face. ''Remember to point the top of your head down into the pool.''

''You forgot something,'' said Anna.

Otis frowned. ''What?''

''Have fun!'' Anna laughed and gave Otis a little shove.

Otis grinned. ''Good one, Anna.''

Walter looked up at all the people watching from the bleachers. ''Aren't you nervous?'' he asked her. Walter remembered how nervous he got standing up in class or in a baseball game when he was up at bat.

Anna shrugged. ''Coach says have a good time and try my best.''

"He's right," said Otis.

Walter and Otis helped Anna find her place. The pool was roped into six lanes. Anna was in lane four. Walter helped Anna put on her swimming goggles.

Anna started talking to a boy named Brian in the lane next to her.

"Don't get friendly with the competition," Walter whispered to Anna.

Anna hooked an arm around Brian. "We're in the same class."

Brian looked down at Anna's feet. "Nice socks," he said.

"My lucky socks!" shouted Walter. He had forgotten all about them.

Anna took them off just in time.

Grandpa Walt stood on one side of the pool. He spoke through a big megaphone. "Swimmers, take your marks!" he announced.

Anna stepped to the edge of the pool.

"Get ready!" boomed Grandpa Walt.

Anna leaned over, ready to dive. She looked straight ahead.

"GO!"

Anna threw her arms forward and pushed off in a strong dive.

Otis jumped up and down. "Way to go, Anna!"

Walter got so excited he tossed his lucky socks in the air. Two weeks ago he didn't think Anna could do anything but belly flop.

Anna and Brian quickly pulled ahead of the other swimmers. They reached the end of the pool. They turned and started back.

"Come on, Anna!" shouted Walter.

"Ann-a! Ann-a! Ann-a!" chanted Otis.

Anna and Brian were swimming side by side. As they neared the finish line the crowd cheered.

Suddenly Brian stopped swimming. His goggles had slid down around his neck. He grabbed a float on the dividing rope. He struggled to push his goggles back up.

"She's gonna win!" screamed Otis.

With Brian out of the race Anna was sure to win.

Anna saw her friend in trouble and stopped. She grabbed the rope and helped Brian with his goggles.

A girl in lane two swam past them both.

Otis and Walter groaned. They watched as Anna swam behind the girl in lane two to the finish line. Anna came in second; Brian, third.

Everyone in the bleachers rose to their feet and cheered. Otis gave Anna a hand out of the pool. She stood smiling at the cheering crowd.

Otis gave her a big hug. "Nice going, Anna."

"That was great, Anna," said Walter, with a handshake. "You should have won."

Grandpa Walt rushed up and gave Anna a bear hug. "She did win," he said. "Right, Anna?"

Anna smiled at Grandpa Walt. "Right."

"But she could have won first place," said Walter.

"You don't have to come in first to be a winner," said Grandpa Walt. "Anna came in second *and* helped her friend Brian. Now, *that's* a winner."

Walter looked at Anna and Brian toweling off. They looked as happy as if they'd both won first place.

After lunch the swimming races continued. Finally it was time to give out awards. Everyone crowded around the awards stands.

"Anna's award is coming up," Grandpa Walt said to Walter. "You better find her."

Walter looked everywhere. Finally he knocked on the door of the girls' room. "Anna, are you in there?"

The door swung open and Anna stepped out.

Walter grabbed her hand. "Come on. They're about to announce your award."

The girl from lane two was already on the

first-place stand in the center. Anna stepped up next to her. Brian stood on the other side.

"First place for ten- to twelve-year-olds in the freestyle event goes to Claudia Simms!" said the announcer.

Grandpa Walt hung a blue-and-yellow ribbon with a gold medal around Claudia's neck.

"Anna's next," Walter whispered to Otis.

"Second place goes to Anna Brink!" said the announcer.

"Yay!" cheered Walter.

Grandpa Walt stepped up to Anna and hung a silver medal around her neck. "Congratulations, Champ," he said.

Brian got a bronze medal for third place. Then Walter and Otis helped hand out ribbons to the winners in fourth, fifth, and sixth places. Every athlete got a medal or a ribbon.

"How about a picture of our star swimmer with her assistant coaches?" said Grandpa Walt. He took a photo of Walter and Otis standing on either side of Anna. They were both smiling and pointing to Anna's silver medal.

Mrs. Howard came down from the bleachers. "Good job, coaches," she said, shaking Walter's and Otis's hands. Walter felt like he'd won a medal too.

Everyone went outside for the Closing Ceremony. They watched the torchbearer put out the Flame of Hope. Then Anna and most of the athletes and volunteers got ready for the special dinner and the victory dance.

The Never Sink Nine friends came down from the bleachers to congratulate Walter and Otis.

Walter blew his whistle. "Time to go to the Pizza Palace."

"All aboard Coach's car!" said Otis, and he blew his whistle.

CHAPTER SEVEN

Before and After

Everyone crowded around a big table in the Pizza Palace.

Grandpa Walt sat down. "I need some pizza. Whose turn is it to order?" They always took turns choosing pizza toppings.

"Mine," said Walter. He raced to the pizza counter and looked at a large gooey pizza with a thick crust. It was covered with extra cheese and extra sausage. "I'll take that one," he said, pointing.

"That'll fatten you up, Walter," said Mrs. Minelli. She owned the Pizza Palace.

Walter looked back at Otis. "Wait," he said. "Do you have a pizza that's not fattening?"

"How about our Diet Deluxe with low-fat cheese and veggies?" said Mrs. Minelli.

Walter nodded. He looked at the big gooey pizza he had wanted. Sometimes being a good friend was hard work.

"Here it is," said Mrs. Minelli, handing the diet pizza to Walter. "Nutritious and delicious."

Walter brought the pizza back to their table. Everyone grabbed a piece.

Pete Santos lifted a green vegetable off the top. "Is this *broccoli*?"

Mike took a bite. "Not bad. What kind of pizza is it?"

"It's the Diet Deluxe," said Walter.

"Good choice," said Grandpa Walt. "We athletes have to stay in shape."

"So do we ballerinas," said Christy.

Otis leaned over toward Walter. "Thanks," he whispered.

66

Tony Pappas opened his drawing pad and pulled out a piece of paper. "Look." He held it up. "It's my first issue of the *Rockville Rookie Report*." It read NEVER SINK NEWS. "It's about Walter and Otis helping with Special Olympics. And here's my *Sidelines* comic strip."

Otis smiled. "Nice. Thanks, Tony."

"I'm going to cover soccer tryouts in the next issue," said Tony.

"My dad's coaching soccer this year," said Mike.

Everyone talked about soccer tryouts until it was time to go.

Grandpa Walt drove everyone home. Walter and Otis sat up front with him.

"This is for you," said Otis, dropping a book in Walter's lap.

Walter read the title: *Stargazing for Beginners*. He opened it to a page filled with stars and planets.

"Mostly pictures," Otis whispered in Walter's ear. "You'll get a gold star for sure."

"Hooper house!" announced Grandpa Walt, pulling into Otis's driveway. Otis hopped out.

"Thanks for the book!" Walter shouted as they drove away.

Walter pulled his lucky socks out of his pocket and put them on. It felt good to have them back.

"I'm proud of you, Slugger," said Grandpa Walt. "It takes a good coach to loan out his lucky socks."

Walter leaned against Grandpa Walt. He was glad he was always the last one to be dropped off. He opened Otis's book again and traced the Big Dipper with a finger.

"Sometimes reaching for the stars means reaching out to a friend," said Grandpa Walt, pulling into the driveway.

"You mean like this?" Walter reached around Grandpa Walt's neck and gave him a hug.

"You've got the idea, Slugger," said Grandpa Walt.

Walter grabbed his backpack and Otis's book and got out of the car.

"Good luck with soccer tryouts!" Grandpa Walt said, driving off.

"Thanks!" shouted Walter.

He looked up at the sky. It was already getting dark. After dinner he would show Danny the Big Dipper. With Otis's book, maybe they could even find the stars that make a bear.

ABOUT THE AUTHOR

GIBBS DAVIS was born in Milwaukee, Wisconsin, and graduated from the University of California at Berkeley. She has published *Swann Song*, a young adult novel, with Avon Books and *The Other Emily* with Houghton Mifflin. *Walter's Lucky Socks, Major-League Melissa, Slugger Mike, Pete the Magnificent, Tony's Double Play, Christy's Magic Glove,* and *Olympic Otis* are all part of the Never Sink Nine series for First Skylark. Gibbs divides her time between New York City and Wisconsin.

ABOUT THE ILLUSTRATOR

GEORGE ULRICH was born in Morristown, New Jersey, and received his Bachelor of Fine Arts degree from Syracuse University. He has illustrated several Bantam Skylark books, including *Make Four Million Dollars by Next Thursday!* by Stephen Manes and *The Amazing Adventure of Me, Myself, and I* by Jovial Bob Stine. He lives in Marblehead, Massachusetts, with his wife and two sons.